First published by Allen & Unwin in 2016

Allen & Unwin – Australia
83 Alexander Street, Crows Nest NSW 2065, Australia
Phone: (61 2) 8425 0100
Email: info@allenandunwin.com
Web: www.allenandunwin.com

Allen & Unwin – UK
Ormond House, 26–27 Boswell Street,
London WC1N 3JZ, UK

A Cataloguing-in-Publication entry is available from the National Library of Australia www.trove.nla.gov.au. A catalogue record for this book is available from the British Library

ISBN (AUS) 978 1 76011 163 2
ISBN (UK) 978 1 74336 806 0

Teachers' notes available from www.allenandunwin.com

Lyrics on pp 5 & 46 from 'In the Good Old Summer Time' written by Ren Shields, 1902
Lyrics on pp 6–7 from 'Give My Regards to Broadway' written by George M. Cohen, 1904
Text Image pp 34–35: Getty Images/APIC – North-East view from Empire State Building by night on the Chrysler Building, New York, 1941

Cover & text design by Tohby Riddle & Megan Pigott
Set in Cooper Bold by Megan Pigott

This book was printed in December 2015 by Hang Tai Printing Company Limited, China

10 9 8 7 6 5 4 3 2 1

www.tohby.com

MILO

a moving story

Tohby Riddle

ALLEN&UNWIN
SYDNEY · MELBOURNE · AUCKLAND · LONDON

For Airlie Riddle

MILO led an ordinary life.
He lived in a solid kennel in an okay part of town
and had few complaints.

Friends often visited Milo – like Cluffy and Snombo.

They got up to all kinds of fun.

And when they couldn't get together,
they used other ways to keep in touch.

Give my regards to Broadway

Remember me to Herald Square

Tell all the gang at Forty-Second Street
That I will soon be there

Every other day, Milo worked as a messenger.

He knew some
very good
shortcuts.

Sometimes his job even took him across town.

Now, one night
Milo had a dream.

He dreamed he was in a little boat being tossed
about on a strange stormy sea.

He didn't sleep well at all.

The next morning, Milo felt cranky and unsettled.
Not even his cup of tea soothed him.

Snombo dropped by. Milo liked Snombo – he'd known him since they were pups – but Snombo had been writing some really lofty poetry and was going on and on about it . . .

Beyond oceans azure
I hear thy distant strains...

Milo tried not to
become irritated . . .

But soon it was like
he had bull ants in
his head!

He almost felt good as he yelled things at Snombo.

AND ANOTHER THING ...
WHY CAN'T YOU JUST ...

Though not long after Snombo had slunk away,
Milo felt really bad.

Milo's day would only get more out of kilter.

A light breeze – no more than a zephyr – picked up.

Mid-afternoon, a largish rabble of moths fluttered by.
Milo had never seen such a thing.

A paper bag sailed over
his kennel . . .

followed by a
blue balloon.

A man scurried by
chasing his hat.

Then a scarecrow flew past.

The breeze had become a wind,
which grew stronger by the minute . . .

Bump! Bump! Bump!

until it was really blowing a gale.

Night was a bumpy ride. A wild ruckus
of wind and noise raged around Milo's kennel.

Huddled inside, Milo fell in and out of a fitful sleep.
He dreamed again that he was in a small boat on
a stormy sea.

Only this time whenever he awoke he felt seasick . . .

Finally, the long night was over. And with its passing came a peaceful dawn.

But something didn't feel right to Milo.
For starters, his kennel seemed to be listing to port and a small cloud had wandered inside.

Shooing the cloud out,
Milo made an important
discovery . . .

His kennel had moved
during the night.

How quickly Milo's life
had changed.

He remembered his argument with Snombo
and sighed. Then he remembered
the moths . . . the scarecrow . . .
and the bumpy night.

As the hours
passed, Milo
pondered
his plight . . .

or just howled softly
to himself.

Then, as luck would
have it, Milo had a
visitor. A migrating bird
stopped by on its way
to Tierra del Fuego.

It had already travelled
a long way, mixing flying
with walking (hence the
comfy sneakers), and had
chosen this out-of-the-way
spot for a rest.

By acting as a counterweight,
the bird, whose name was Carlos,
helped Milo to safer ground.

Carlos was a mostly unremarkable bird, though he did have a few display feathers he could show if he needed to impress anyone.

It was also unusual for migratory birds to walk parts of their journey. But as Carlos often said: 'I like walking. You see so much more when you go by foot.'

High above the glittering metropolis, Carlos and Milo spent the night swapping stories, songs, ideas . . .

Milo realised it was a big wide world out there.

Come morning,
a window-cleaner
showed up for
a day's work.

He made an offer.
If Milo helped wash
windows, he'd take his
kennel to the ground.
Milo agreed.

Carlos agreed too – just
for the fun of it. He said
he liked to have different
experiences on his travels.

Once on the ground, they farewelled the window-cleaner.

Then they fashioned a trolley so they could tow the kennel back to where it belonged.

In the meantime, Milo's friends had gathered around the spot where his kennel had been. Even Snombo.

They feared the worst.

It was relief all round when Milo appeared,
towing his kennel behind him.

And they could hardly believe Milo's strange tale
of peril and survival on the roof of the city itself.

With everything back in its rightful place, a celebration was in order.

It was a happy occasion, though Milo noticed Snombo was still a bit sniffy.

Milo wished with all his heart that he could take his words back.
He said sorry to Snombo. As he spoke, Snombo looked sad,
perhaps even a little angry – but mostly sad.

That night, Milo dreamed that he was in
a little boat again, but the sea was calm
and land was in sight.

Milo slept long and well, and woke feeling much more like his usual self. Isn't life a mystery, he thought.

With the birds in the trees-es
And sweet scented breezes,
Good old summer time...

Two days later, he had a parcel to deliver.
On his way out he noticed something on his doorstep.

It was a bound collection of Snombo's poetry and a biscuit.